Rush

Of

Many

Waters

Also by Pauly Hart

Novels:
By the Gates of the Garden of Eden
Novellas:
Superior Respondent
Ouesso to Epena
The Book of Lesser Voices
Mountain to Mountain
The Word of Yahweh unto Enoch
Empire of the Dragon
Finance:
The Richest Man In Babylon Continued Stories
Collections:
Sometimes I Write Tiny Stories
Adelphoi
Poetry:
Stupid Mind Tricks
Book of Love and Laughter
The Cross and the Poet
What is Poep?
I Love You More Than a Fox Loves Blueberries
The Night Clerk Held a Broken Pencil
Spontaneous Psalms
Kick the Prick
Exegesis with Co-Authors:
My Flat Earth
Biblical Cosmology, 8+ languages
Translations:
The Testament of Job in Modern English
Children's:
Mathmagician and Other Tales of Awesomeness
Periodicals:
Modern Epistle (1-8)
Microzine (1-5)
Rush of Many Waters (1-20)
With children authors:
Farrell Family Fables
With Co-Author Jennifer Hart:
Adulting: A Daily Guide on Being an Adultier Adult
Audiobooks:
Biblical Cosmology
Superior Respondent

Rush of Many Waters:

Volume Six

By Pauly Hart

Contents

Shorts

The End of Summer Camp

You really shouldn't be reading this absurd story, cause I think I should be locked away, but the more I ask people to lock me away, the more medication they give me and tell me to stay at home. Anyway, in case you are reading this at all, I'll tell you all about this crazy summer and all the weird things that happened. I really don't want to, but my dad thought it would be a great way for me to "exercise the healing process" or whatever… I'm sure my dad means well but he's never been much of a helpful guy anyway, since he's always so busy with his business, but the therapist he's making me go to agrees with him (Mrs. Kelso, if you're reading this, I'm pretty sure you know everything in this that I'm going to say anyway, but whatever). I'm going to tell you all about it anyway, just in case some notes or transcripts or whatever get lost due to nuclear disaster or whatever. Hey, I don't ever expect nuclear disaster but I know that sometimes they talk about it on the news so it never hurts to be prepared, right?

So I used to work at a camp for crippled children. If you can imagine a place in the woods where the rich well to-do adult types send their children to go have fun swimming in a lake, shooting with bow and arrows, and climbing walls; you can imagine the kind of place I mean. It was a crazy happy place, and things were pretty swell – it was the middle of the season and this was one of the only jobs I ever liked. Most camps like this were week-to-week things, where at the end of every week you shed some hot tears for the little lives you've attached your horrible heart to, and then they leave, back to their little summer selves… You feel bad for about a day, and do a lot of yard work or whatever to clean the camp back up and then a new batch of ruffians unload off the bus and you do it all over again. But the summer camp I worked at wasn't a week-to-week camp; this was an all-summer camp. This was a place where the little tikes could form a friendship that lasted the rest of their silly lives. I mean, really, the name of the place, the size of the place, even what we had for dessert on Tuesdays doesn't matter now; the whole thing was destroyed in a horrific lake accident. Wait. I'm getting ahead of myself.

Ok. I'll begin for real. Just for posterity and giggles: Camp Summerville was the name of the place. It was in the woods, near a lake, in the Upper Peninsula in Michigan where you could pay $35,500 to send your child for two months so you could go on your way gallivanting around the world in your private jet or whatever it is rich people do... But yeah. There we were. Oh. By "we" I mean, the camp staff and the children and the groundskeepers and the kitchen people and all of them... You know, regular people at a camp. So, I worked there as a counselor, if you have to know - Which I think you do have to know for this story to make sense - but anyway. It was around the fourth of July... No, yeah, it was the fourth, at the night time campfire. All the guys who ran the camp had called it "Jamboree" even though that name is trademarked by the Boys Scouts of America, and they could get into some serious trouble, but whatever, it was just a big sweaty fire at night where we all sang songs about friendship and coming to Jesus and laughed at all the stupid skits we did.

July 4th Jamboree - there we were, stealing Boy Scout trademarks and everything... The counselors had practiced their "Stand up America" skit the weekend before and it was set to a really powerful soundtrack by Ennio Morricone or Hans Zimmer or John Williams or one of those ubermasters. The song was: "Sing your song, true believer" and it didn't fit with the "America" thing so much as it centered on faith, but whatever, I suppose patriotism and nationalism are sort of a by-product of Americana worship anyway, but what did I know? I was seventeen and full of gonadotrophic hormones dancing around my stupid seventeen year-old brain. Hell, I saw more boobies in bathing suits than should be legal in any state. But anyways, I was singing to Jesus, or the children, or the owls and bats that circled above us, eating wandering June-bugs... When I kinda felt it. "Sing your song, true believer, sing your song, don't be scared!" Went the song, but in my heart It felt like black talons screeching on a chalk-board. Not the song... It was a really awesome song, but the feeling was weird. The feeling was off. Way off. I mean, who the hell feels something like that when you're singing such a glad and happy tune? Not me. Well, I mean, it was really exactly me, but you know what I mean.

So in the skit, we're all dressed up with the old red white and blue makeup and wearing cowboy hats and hardhats and all the other hats the Village People wore and are dressed as soldiers and businessmen and (obviously) cowboys and construction workers, and we sing and march around and then pivot at the very end and salute the flag. I wouldn't really call it a skit, as it was more of mime-lock-step-marching, if your brain can imagine such a thing. And so Janice, the pretty Janice obviously, is supposed to walk in front of me and do a fake trust fall in the middle of the song, just to keep the action going. Well, you know Janice had on that top that I couldn't keep my eyes off; her whole body was somehow patriotic enough to just be painted with a partial flag underneath a really spiffy bikini top. Super spiffy, and I almost dropped her when she did the trust fall, cause all I was watching were her two girls... Hey, they were nice girls. Just the right height from neck to belly button and anyways, I'm seventeen and had a mind of mud and was still a virgin so there was this feeling that I got right then and there, that the whole thing was really awful, and it had nothing to do with Janice.

Just a feeling, but like I said, it was like dark talons screeching on some dark chalkboard in the bellows of hell, or gates of hell. Classrooms of hell? Where would you keep a chalkboard in hell anyways? I can imagine the whole kosmokrator in their classrooms learning how to be little good demons and all saying the pledge of allegiance to Satan with a "Sieg Heil Satan" salute every morning. Maybe like Germans? Sorry German children everywhere, I don't really want to compare you to demons, but I still remember the old films from when I was a little minion myself. Anyway, I almost dropped Janice right then and there and she wasn't too happy with it all, but then again, I never told her about the German demons salute either, so I figured it would all be ok. Heck, if I did tell her about them, what kind of a guy would she think I was anyway? Some kind of crazy lunatic? Probably.

The feeling came and went as quickly as that, so there I was finishing up the whole patriotism thing on a sweaty stage with bats and owls eating mosquitos over my head and I had to salute some crazy flag dressed up like a modern day businessman. Oh yeah, but it was just a hat and a tie and my swim trunks. I was painted like a flag too. A flag saluting a flag on the fourth of July. You can't get more demented than that, right? But I did, and we finished, and then we just stood there like fools while Chuck, the camps big shot owner who ran everything, came out and gave an altar call to be "righteous in the land" or somesuch. We were supposed to sit down, or go to our benches, but since I was the first towards the flag, I just stood there like a statue in full salute, even though I wasn't even wearing any uniform. There was probably something illegal in the whole ordeal, I didn't even have my Boy Scout totin' chit in my wallet. Heck, I didn't even have my wallet on me; I was in my swimming trunks.

Chuck was fervently talking about a guy named Nehemiah and the builders of some wall somewhere when Jake tapped me on the shoulder and I turned around. All of the other counselors had sat down. He was my bunk mate counselor and he waved his hand to say: "Get off the stage you moron." I looked around and it was just me, saluting. How long had I been the only one on the stage saluting? Maybe ten years. Felt like it. I ducked down to the grins and looks of the other counselors and evil German demon children. Like some dumb balloon head, I went back to my seat with the couple of miniature humans who hadn't gone forward in the America Jesus altar call to be a good upstanding citizen for their motherland. Fatherland? Whicheverland it was, I wasn't convinced that I wanted to have any part of their vaccinated calcified pineal gland mind programming... So I sat there and thought about it all.

It wasn't anything crazy or anything like a brain aneurism or that kinda thing, believe me, I'd know if I had a brain aneurism or something, but it was the weirdest thing, like, imagine a window opens up into another dimension and you peer in on a woman and her family eating salad and they had a salmon on in the middle of the table and you can tell that the children don't want to eat a crummy salad when they could be tucking into that big old fish. And the woman has on a yellow flower print dress and the guy has on some sort of corn-flower blue V-neck sweater vest and the children are all swell and the whole scene is 1953 Leave-it-to-Beaver and you can almost hear the laugh track and smell the salmon and then suddenly the window is slammed shut but then you got just the faintest whiff of Salmon and it drives you nuts. It was like that, this feeling. But it wasn't Ward Cleaver and company, it was demons.

So that's what I thought about on the way back, making the children brush their teeth and go to bed and quit talking and then I went out on the back porch to sit and stare at the moon. It was a super moon and Jake came outside and shot the breeze for a minute and then left me alone staring at the moon thinking about demons and chalkboards. I went to bed a little later, forgetting to brush my teeth, obviously because they tasted like Spanish Moss when I woke up but then again, we were going to eat breakfast in a little bit anyway so I popped my brush in my pocket as Jake and I and our nine 12 year old heathens marched down to the mess hall for waffles and gravy, cheesy grits, turkey bacon and a wide variety of sugary American cold breakfast cereals.

The way that summer counselors who have bunk children works is that they teach the classes during the day and then sometimes there's other duties during the day. My first job was bunk inspector, so Tina (one of the girl counselors) and I walked around to all the cabins looking at how messy or dirty they were. There was a prize each week for the cleanest cabins and it always went to the girls. They would leave little candies and mints and sometimes cookies to bribe us, so I was always munching away. Jake and I never cared about our cabin and we usually won the last place which always meant a pie to the face, which was kind of fun so we just kept being last. Our little minions got into the swing of things too and we would make it messier on purpose. We came to our cabin and I said to skip it and Tina and I moved on, almost grateful that we didn't have to go in. Well, I didn't care. All the gratefulness was on her end. You could even smell the funk of our mess just by walking by. Chuck had talked to Jake and me about how messy we were and kinda got onto our cases, but he didn't fire us, so it didn't really matter, we still worked there, right?

And there was that crawling on the back of my neck right as we were coming to cabin #14, one of the girl's cabins. I can't remember who the counselors were for this one, but it wasn't the girl I was with… It was the unique one… Oh yeah, Eunique was her name. Yeah. The one with the unique spelling of "unique" - Eunique, which really bugged me a lot, because obviously the joke was on her, someone else on the world would have thought to spell their daughter's name the wrong way, making it more unique than "unique" which was just the opposite of unique, because any object, or spelling that was not in itself on its own accord, specifically one of a kind, was no longer unique. And that make me think of that crazy guy who wrote some intergalactic hitchhiking guide comedy series or something… I couldn't remember his name but his characters… The guy who designed the fiords or Norway or something, his name was Slartibartfast. Now that was a unique name, because I had never met one of those guys before, I would remember it. Wait a minute. Dang. Now that there was a guy who wrote about that name, would someone else write it too? Yeah, probably some dumb nerd would name his dog that name and it would no longer be unique. What a shame for that dumb dog named Slartibartfast.

They left us Watermelon Jolly Ranchers in #14 and a sense of overwhelming dread. There was this really big black banner hung from the ceiling that read: "42 is the name of his reign" written all in this crazy red ink. And all around the cabin, the little girls had made construction paper signs in black that looked like little shields and crowns and all in black with a big red "42" on all of them. It was kinda weird but when I saw the word 42 I think that's what clued me into the whole hitchhiker's book thing, cause I think that was in the book too. I shuddered cause I was suddenly super cold and tripped out by all of this creepy nonsense, but Tina told me to quit being stupid, but with three Jolly Ranchers in my mouth, I just shrugged. Cabin #14 was the winner that day, but we couldn't tell anyone about it, and it was time for second period anyway. I had to teach beginner's swimming. I think I got stuck with the crap jobs because I was the least helpful or least experienced person there. I was seventeen but all I had done in the past was scoop ice-cream as a job... Oh sure, I had gone to a camp as a child in the middle of the Kansas desert and shoveled horse poop from the stalls and done some babysitting, but I don't think that qualified me to teach the rock climbing wall, or the high altitude ropes course. I got to teach beginner's swimming.

That was fine. We had eight or nine children in the class, and since this was week five, all of them were doing alright, except for Melissa. There was the other instructor, Emily, and she spent a lot of time with Melissa, but I think it was sort of a codependent thing, because Melissa wouldn't come in the water unless Emily was with her. Melissa had some sort of Muscular Sclerosis and had almost drowned as a baby when her rat-hole dad forced her to swim. So now it was me and the other eight little chimpanzees, splashing around on paddleboards and learning how to float and it was really crazy boring. And even though it was ten in the morning, I still got the feeling that some sort of inky monster would crawl out of the drain and grab my leg and drag me under. Nothing to bother the children about but, you know... Inky monsters who grab your legs should always be guarded against.

Since there was only beginner's class, and the next class was regular swimming, we hustled the beginner children out while the second period started. All goons, they did their thing, while I blew my whistle at runners and chicken fighters. Man was I jealous, sitting in my chair watching these little monsters having all the fun. But before I knew it, it was first break, and we all hustled out of there and ran to the snack shack for our sugar rush of the morning. I didn't have to work it today so that gave me some time to sit around and sponsor the push-up contest for the macho boys. Since I was pretty good at them myself, I would go first and set the standard for the rest of the little body-builder wannabes. All the boys were either having a go at it or looking on. And these were children with muscle diseases and all sorts of stuff wrong with them. One of the boys, as healthy as an ox, but blind as a bat, usually won. I forget his name, but he had that sort of strength that sloths have. He wasn't mentally challenged or anything, but his strength was nuts. He would always do three more than me, and jump up and down after with his hands in the air, like he had just won a prize fight. Little monster.

I didn't have any problems the rest of the morning until lunch, all of the counselors were allowed "down time" in their day to "prepare and rest" and weird words like that. Heck, I'm some random teenager taking care of your crippled children, so it looks great on a brochure to tell the rich folk their counselors are cognizant and aware of their own perceived reality and gravity of the situation and how serious it all is to everyone that Melissa can do the backstroke. Sure, whatever sells the place I suppose. I went to the bunkhouse and took a nap until lunch. But I didn't nap at all. I just lay on some random bunk looking up at the one above me. See, they were all these bunkbeds, so you could cram all 8 little monsters in one bunkhouse and give them the feeling that the ones who couldn't climb didn't need to. Since there were 8 sets, most of the top ones weren't used. We had one little dude, Gilroy, who was weirdly afraid of sleeping too close to the floor and he was the only top bunker, except me. I was on the top on the other side of the room, and the way I faced, all I could see was the forest and the lake. But I lay on one of the other beds right now, just thinking about that feeling and also about the ink monster in the pool.

I didn't want to think about either one, but I didn't really have a choice in the matter, so that's what I did, my crazy brain drifting away to some weird place when someone opened the door and scared the poop right out of me. I wiped my lip from a long string of drool and realized that I must have been asleep. One of the other guy counselors told me that I was late to lunch and that I was doing the cleanup call so I'd better hurry.

The cleanup caller was the unfortunate soul who had the duty to weigh the pig bucket and challenge the little cretins that food wasted was their fault and that we were feeding pigs their food and that they should feel some overwhelming sense of shame and disgust at themselves for allowing the food to go to waste. Now that really got my blood boiling because I knew full well that we fed the pigs anyway, no matter what the children did or did not eat. See, it was served "family style" from the kitchen. One poor soul from each cabin's dinner table was set as a "runner" and went to the kitchen to grab the food on a big tray and serve the table. The food from the tray wasn't counted, but when it hit the child's plate, then they had to eat it or it would go to waste. But that didn't matter because the kitchen cooked the same amount of food, no matter what happened at the table or not... So it was a huge hypocrisy game. A shell game of guilt and confusion set onto the children by the evil overlord Chuck, and his horde (board) of directors.

So I hustled over to the dining hall, grabbed a quick bite of some soup and jumped up to the microphone and proceeded to go thru what they all knew already, that the runner chosen for the day would be the one scooping up the slop and putting it in the bucket, and that at the end of the meal all the plates went in one of the large gray bus tubs and bowls in another. I have no idea why they called them bus tubs or what even bussing a table meant, but that's the jargon that they all used, so I went with it, because "cleaning" sounds pretty awful. So then I pick one random slob from a table to grab the bucket and bring it to the front and weigh it. Well Agnus is the poor fool I chose, because of that awful shirt he wore about how then Scottish Highlands are more important than anything else and here it was, July the 5th and he couldn't find a better shirt to wear than to beat up on the old U. S. of A.

We were at a pound and a half of slop that lunch, and it was all fine and good for them because we beat our old record of a pound and three quarters and I made a big deal of it all and that was lunch and I had to go shovel horse poop... The same job I had as a little rancher, so many years ago now... Man, was it ten years ago? I guess that's all I was good for, ten years ago was shoveling. "Ranch Hand" they called it, but I never touched the horses, except to help people on and off anyway. It was grooming day so no one was riding, and I helped hold the bridle so they could all take turns brushing the horse. One of the demons brushing a tame old mare named "Rosey" was really giving it a go and trying to make Rosey bald on her left gaskin. That's the left back forearm... Don't ask me why they get "arm" from anything, it's not like a horse builds their own fences, with four legs and all... But Rosey was getting a little annoyed so I had to show the little terrorist how to be gentle. Marcia, the main horse lady was there and stepped in as well. Being gentle was Marcia's specialty. The horses loved her and knew her and she was pretty cute, for an old lady.

So two periods of that and it was second snack shack time where cold water was the drink of choice for me. None of that sugar stuff now, not in the heat. It would make me wooze out and feel all crumbly. Then off to rest period, which was a joke, because after snack shack #2, the monkeys were bouncing off the walls, throwing flashlights across the room, batteries flying everywhere, but pretty soon, they crashed out and were sleeping and I went to the back deck to get away from it all. I didn't get very far because Jake wanted to talk about Tina so I just left and told him I would meet him at all-camp games, which was directly after rest period, in around an hour. All-Camp Games was a pretty cool invention of somebody a long time ago where we would have sort of a miniature Olympics and we did it every other week or so, whenever we ran out of other stuff to do. That's the thing about camp… You never have can have too much planned, because you never know about emergencies and stuff like that.

But it seemed like an eternity as I walked along the lake, thinking about the evil forces at work in my imagination, or maybe, in reality. What in the holy heckfire had I seen or glimpsed or felt during the sketch? What in the world was it? Maybe it was just in my imagination. Anyway, the lake was calm as usual. The geese who had infested the back corner had been driven off by old Crusty, the lake-keeper. He was a mean old sod and didn't allow himself to get any guff from any of us counselors or even from Chuck. His family was the original owners of the place, some crazy old Catholic thing - Knights of Malta or something like that, and I guess had a crazy long lease to the camp for a hundred years or something. I guess the old place used to be some sort of retreat for the old Knights, which I didn't really think they were, by the way… I mean, were they really walking around here in shining armor and all that King Arthur stuff anyways? So old Crusty would be out there, with his little boat, dumping weird stuff from barrels into it, and people left him alone. Right before camp started, he had a bunch of dudes out there, dredging up a lot of the moss and slime and goo that hung out on the bottom. It was really zany to watch, he would yell and scream and bicker about the drainage lines and the sacred cairn cap at the bottom. That's all I know… Those were words he used, not that I knew anything about sacred cairn caps at the bottom of lakes or anything. But he was dang sure to yell at everyone working for him to let them know about that dang old whatever it was.

And now there he was hollering at something in the water and pulled out a big old bronze rifle and shot at it. What in the world was he thinking shooting the water like that? But he was cursing, standing up in that little blue rowboat with all the herons flying like crazed maniacs getting the heck out of there because Old Crusty was shooting stuff again. *Bang,* another shot into the water and he was standing up like a professional surfer going at it with the big waves of Hawaii or something. *Bang,* shooting it again and cussing up such a storm, reloading his gun after two more bangs. That mean old rifle just waited, barrel smoking until he popped in another five shots into the little magazine and he went after it cussing with each shot.

The even more bizarre thing was that cabin #14 was glowing like some sort of a Halloween carnival furnace. And the fact that Eunique was standing out on the porch with her arms raised and there were little flashes of lightning dancing from her fingertips, didn't help lower the bar any. I didn't even have time to think about it as Old Crusty was still doing the jig on the little boat right in front of me. Dodging left and right he sat down quick and rowed a little over passed the middle and stood up again and took another shot. This was in the space of, oh, who knows, maybe three minutes, but it might as well have been a hundred years, cause by this time, all the children and counselors were out on the back decks looking down at the water and at Old Crusty, loading the rifle again. *Boom!* The loudspeaker crackled on and Chuck told everyone to go back inside. A couple of the girls' bunks did, but all the boys' bunks were getting a show. From where they were looking, they saw the lake, Old Crusty, and me, on the other side, just eyeballing the scene like madmen.

Chuck came gunning down the little road towards me in his blue golf-cart. That little thing was faster than the other golf carts at camp; it had some real pick-up-and-go to it. Dang. The golf cart I used could only go half that speed, man was he flying, and now he's all yelling at me and stuff to go back inside. No wait, now he's yelling at me to get on the cart with him while Old Crusty fires off another volley into the abyss. There's a huge splash and dang Crusty wasn't there anymore. There was a huge *kersplosh* and Chuck slams on the brakes causing the cart to skid out on the asphalt and almost hit me. We both look out at the lake and see a huge purple vine growing over Old Crusty's little boat and there's another vine and then the boat snaps in half and then there's no more boat.

Dang.

Crazy Chuck is also packing, as weird as it sounds, and it's a "Come-to-Jesus" moment for purple vine thing, as it inches under the water like a Sturgeon on a mission. Maybe a Walleye. Those suckers can get pretty big. Oh a catfish can get bigger, but they always just hang out on the bottom looking for free stuff. A nasty Sturgeon can take you down if you're not ready. And that's what it looked like, until this gigantic head pushed out from the middle of the lake, and I swear on my Aunt Tiffany's China set, it was some crazy huge cat. But by then it was too late for Chuck, cause he fired at the thing six times but nothing happened, except poor Chuck's eyes were as big as saucers when last I saw them, being sucked underwater by those vine things. And then that's when I hopped into the golf cart and boogied away like a madman.

I reached into my pocket and pulled out my toothbrush when she began honking. I don't remember walking, but I guess I must have been doing so for a while because the lady in the red pickup was yelling at me to get out of the road. I don't know where the golf-cart was, or even where I was, but that was ok because I wasn't near camp any more. Man, when one of those purple vines looked at me sideways, I didn't want to stick around to say hello. I guess Old Crusty didn't say hello too nicely or even Chuck but the lady in the red truck was nice to me and took me to town. I called my parents and told them to come pick me up because I didn't want to be a camp counselor anymore.

Elizabeth was six years old. She liked all sorts of things but she really, really liked ice cream. Rainbow flavored is the best. It really doesn't taste like rainbows though. She wondered how a rainbow really did taste. She loved dogs too, but thought that rainbow flavored ice cream should win some sort of an award on one of those TV shows. Dogs should win too; Maybe rainbow ice cream should be full of sparks and fluffy marshmallows. She wondered if dogs liked rainbows. She didn't know how sparks tasted, and didn't want to eat firecrackers. She knew how marshmallows tasted. Marshmallows are yummy. She licked the ice cream on her fingers. Ice cream was great. This was the best ice cream in the world.

"Not with your tongue sweetheart" her mom said. "Use a napkin."

"Why? I'll lose it that way! Plus, it makes my hand sweet for when I pet Patches."

Her mom scowled and put the napkin down. Their dog, Patches, would make sure that her hands were clean. Elizabeth really, really loved that dog. Her mom sighed and ate more Butter Brickle. She said it reminded her of when Granddad used to take her for ice cream. Elizabeth thought Butter Brickle tasted like wet socks. She didn't really know what that meant, but it sounded funny. It was something that her friend Jennifer's dad said all the time.

"Why couldn't dad come too?" Elizabeth asked, her thoughts on her own dad.

"Uh. Because he doesn't live with us anymore, remember honey?" Her mom said. That was still so confusing. "Now eat that side before it falls off." Her mom said.

Elizabeth sighed. Her mom thought she was still just a baby.

Elizabeth didn't care about all the things her mom had told her about being a good little girl. She knew she wasn't a baby anymore, because baby stuff was silly. She really wanted to be an astronaut when she grew up. Her bottom two teeth had fallen out. Besides, she could eat ice cream all by herself. She missed her dad. This really was the best ice cream in the whole world.

Her mom said it was time to go. "Time to go."

"One more scoop?" Elizabeth asked. Her mom frowned. "We can save it for later. Put it in a cup!" She knew her mom would do it.

"No honey, we need to get going." Her mom gave a stupid excuse. Her mom always had stupid excuses.

"But I want a scoop for later for when I'm tired and hungry." Elizabeth said, mournfully.

"When you're tired and hungry, then it's probably time to go to sleep." Her mom said.

Elizabeth didn't want to go. Elizabeth wanted more rainbow ice cream. More ice cream. More! She wanted it now, and she would get her way.

"No!" She threw her unfinished cone on the ground and slammed her palms on the table. "I want more Rainbow ice cream for later!" She screamed almost at the top of her lungs.

Her mom's eyes went really big and all the color left her face. But right at that instant Elizabeth didn't care. She wanted this so badly, like she'd never wanted anything in her entire life... Ever.

The people at the little ice cream shop inside heard her scream through the glass, and the other couples sitting outside really, really heard her. She looked at her mom with the biggest frown she could make. "Right now mother." she said.

That really worked. She had never called mom that word before, but her mom went inside and almost threw money at the man behind the counter, and brought out a little bag.

"Grab my hand. We're going home and we're going to have a nice discussion." Her mother had her purse and her bag in her left hand and stuck her right arm down with her fingers way out. She reminded Elizabeth of the pelicans at the zoo.

"Fine," Elizabeth said, grabbing her hand. Her mom almost dragged her to the car, the way Elizabeth sometimes did with her dolls.

Neither one spoke on the way home. That was fine with Elizabeth. She kept looking over at the white bag with the ice cream inside. She wanted it so badly, it was like it was Christmas morning.

When they got home, she ran into the house and ran to her room. She knew that's what her mom would say to her anyway, she just didn't want to hear it. She slammed the door and started walking around in circles. Ice cream. Ice cream. Ice cream. Her brain was on fire. She wanted more of that ice cream.

Very slowly she opened her door to listen. Her mom was outside smoking but she was on the phone with her friend Jennifer's mom. Usually she didn't care when her mom talked about her, but she shouldn't talk to her friend's moms. That was mean.

She went downstairs as fast as she could, and went to the freezer. No ice cream? What? She looked on the kitchen table. No, it wasn't on the table. Where was it? Where was...

Her mom had thrown it away. It was in the trash.

Her mom would pay.

Grabbing a spoon from the drawer, she ran upstairs as fast as she could. As she was at the top of the stairs she heard the pool gate door slam shut and then the sliding glass door opened and her mom's voice... Like it was her regular voice. Her mom was still talking.

"And the thing of it was that she never acts like this, ever! And guess what? Huh?... Yes!... No!... She called me: 'mother' of all things! Has Jenny ever said that before? Ever... Yes... Oh! I know!" But Elizabeth didn't hear any more. She was in the room with the Rainbow ice cream from the trash.

She had a strange idea to lock the door, but she had never done that before. She tried the little button and it clicked when she pushed it. There, she was locked in the room, and her mom couldn't stop her. No one can open locked doors. Still, she felt like she should also do something else. She got in the closet and shut that door as well. It was dark, but there was a little light from under the door. She opened up the bag, opened up the little container and plunged the spoon in.

Mary hung up with Alison and put the phone down on the table. What in the world had come over her daughter? She has never acted like this! Never! The whole thing was surreal. Not in a million years would she have thought that her daughter could have acted this way... Especially in a public place!

She put the phone down on the table, reluctant to talk to Elizabeth after the fiasco she had caused. She wondered what her grandfather would say about that. Probably give her some Inuit advice about little children behaving in evil ways and being taken away by some watery monster. She laughed at that. There was that one story she remembered about some water demon. Callipoo... Something? Was that it? She picked up her phone and googled it. "Qalupalik." That was it. The green skinned long haired monster that would drag bad children off to sea. She didn't need her grandfather now that she had google, but she still missed his voice.

She sat down, phone still in hand. Qalupalik. Qalupalik. Call-oo-pail-ek. Interesting. She googled some more and found another article about it and still another and then even another one that talked about northern children and their psychological build remaining normalized while trying to break away from tradition. The viewpoints from the US Department of Education were funny though. That they would even care about the indigenous were unsettling. They stole everything and now wanted to help? The topic made her furious. Yuck. US government stuff. Thanks white people.

Still, it was an insightful reveal into her own childhood. She and Elizabeth had moved away when Elizabeth was still a baby, leaving Tim alone in the snowy wasteland that was Barrow, Alaska right after they renamed it. God, she had hated that place. Leaving and taking her daughter with her had been the best decision that she had ever made. God bless Tim, whatever he may be doing now... He's just not doing it with us. She needed another cigarette.

Out on the back stoop she retrieved a pack of Misty Menthol Green 120's from her little hidey-hole. She took one out and lit it with her green Bic. "Green, green, green," she thought to herself. Green is all I want now. Screw Alaska. I'm so done with that place. I hope grandpa lives to be 120 so I don't ever have to go back.

There was a splash out by the pool. Probably one of the neighbor's dogs. She couldn't see the pool directly from the back porch, you had to go out through the gate and round the hedges to get to it. But it was nice that the condo complex was designed in such a way that all of the back doors had access to one of the many pools. She put out her cigarette in the little ashtray and went back indoors.

She shuddered. Qalupalik. Her grandfather had raised her by himself and had told her that story. The green skin really scared her and made her behave. Was it right to lie to children like that? To tell them something wasn't true to frighten them into good behavior? It had worked on her... Until she was seventeen and got pregnant, that is. Tim had been a hotshot snowmobiler, and he had whisked her away with attention and time that no other boy had shown her, and she had let him in her pants.

"Ugh" she said out loud, and hopped on the phone again. She had gone to get ice cream with her Elizabeth to have a good time. She knew about the place from Gloria, a friend she had here in town from Sitka, Alaska. Even though it was southern Alaska and had only half the problems Barrow did, they had become besties very quickly. Talking about winter while you were literally three thousand miles away was refreshing. She laughed. Having another Alaskan friend here in town was a miracle that she could never have prayed for.

Gloria and her husband Lennord were the owners of the ice cream shop. They made everything in the shop by hand from Lennord's family recipes. They were both from Alaska. Lennord was from Kodiak, or maybe farther down the chain, where your whole life is at sea. She called Gloria.

"Hey Gloria." Mary said.

"Hey girl, what's new?" Gloria said.

"Oh nothing. Hey, we were just at your shop and Elizabeth threw the most God-awful fit over your Rainbow Ice cream. It was really weird."

"Is she sick?" Gloria asked.

"Sick?" Mary said, not sure where this was going.

"Yes. Dammit. I told Lennard not to sell it. We get in stuff all the time from his family. They made their own vanilla from the Slender Spire plant and sent it to us. Lennord used it in all the batches of Rainbow."

Slender Spire was technically an orchid, so it could be done. Most people don't know how to extract vanilla, but the Inuit are resourceful. Having a natural plant from Alaska here in Arizona was weird enough, but to have been eaten by a child who was from Alaska... What were the odds?

"Wait." Mary was a little dizzy. "They *made* vanilla?"

"Yes!" Gloria said. "Honey, check on Elizabeth and call me back."

Mary was already going towards the stairs. "I'll just keep you on the phone. Hold on." she said.

When she reached the top of the stairs she heard a *thump* and breaking glass. It came from Elizabeth's room. Going to the door, she tried the handle. It was locked.

"Elizabeth!" Mary yelled. "Open this door at once!"

"What's going on?" Mary heard Gloria yelling on the other end of the phone.

Just then, Elizabeth started screaming.

Try as she might she could not open the door. "Elizabeth!" She screamed at the top of her lungs but all she heard was more screaming and a crash that sounded like her dresser being knocked over. Then Mary heard more glass shattering and Elizabeth's screaming sounded like it was coming from outside.

"Elizabeth!" she cried desperately, working the doorknob back and forth, slamming her shoulder into it. But the glass? Why would Elizabeth have broken glass? Did she break out the window? Was she outside? There was only one way to find out.

Mary raced down the steps at full speed, and out the sliding back door. She looked up at the window. It was broken out and there was glass all over the ground. Why would she go out of the window?

The pool gate clanged shut behind her, behind the bushes. She missed Elizabeth by seconds. Why is she going to the pool?

"Elizabeth!" she screamed.

"Mommy!" Elizabeth screamed back. "Make her stop!"

What the fuck?

There was a large splash.

She rushed out the door and turned toward the pool.

Empty except for...

The briefest glimpse of Elizabeth's legs going into the deep end. "No!" Mary screamed and rushed towards the pool's edge.

She had seen where Elizabeth had gone in. Right here. *Hang on honey, Mommy is going to save you,* she thought. Without thinking, she jumped in feet first, hopefully over her daughter. Elizabeth couldn't swim without floaties.

When she hit, the shock of the water and the strange sensation of having clothing on disoriented her for a few seconds, but she was underwater grasping...

At nothing. She came to the surface and looked around.

There was nothing there. No Elizabeth. Nothing.

She went down again. Turned. Nothing. Turned again... Nothing.

She couldn't see properly here. She got to the edge and pulled herself out and stood looking at the empty pool. She raced around the edge in disbelief.

She had seen her daughter go in! *What in the world?* She flipped her hair back and wiped her eyes scanning the pool back and forth. This was not possible.

She went back to the deep end. She hadn't noticed it before, but there, just at the edge, was Elizabeth's ice cream cup. It was on its side. Mary picked it up. It was still cool. It was also covered in long gray hair.

At the shallow edge of the pool, a lime green floaty sat in the water. Just now being hit with the ripples, it bumped the side of the pool.

Bump.

Bump.

Bump.

Poems

Jeremiah

Oh that my eyes were a river,
Oh that my head was a spring.
I would weep for dying people,
I would weep for the lost king.

Oh that I had in this desert,
a place for the lost and confused.
o I could bring all the lost people,
those hurting, dying and abused.

Will even my Lord come and save me,
Comforter and everything?
My mind is aloof and fainthearted,
does he hear my needs as I sing?

The cry of the lost and the dying,
the cry of the hurt and dismayed.
For I'm in a land that is crying,
we have been snared and enslaved.

But is there no king in our Zion,
is there no king in this land?
The city of peace is forsaken,
the flowers have turned into sand.

Oh, I see the fields of the harvest,
I see them rotting away.
The harvest has passed with the summer,
we have not been saved.

I am poured out like fresh water,

I cry the hours away.
And where is the promise of healing,
while I am still crying all day?

My people are crushed and so I am,
my sorrows and theirs intertwined.
 weep and mourn for the horror,
The fears that are so deep inside.

Where is the promise of healing,
where are the people who care?
Why is there no hope of mending,
why am I filled with despair?

There is no doctor and no hope,
while we are all rotting away.
The harvest is passed and is ended,
and we are still not saved.

And Oh that my eyes were a river!
Oh that my head were a spring!
I would weep for dying people!
I would weep for the lost king!

but am not afraid

I run but am not afraid.
I run into your arms.
I scream but am not afraid.
I explode with laughter.
but am not afraid.
I well up with your joy.
I hide but am not afraid.
I hide within your arms.
I run but am not afraid.

She moves my hand when I touch her
She hits me when I try
She tenses when I talk abruptly
I hate it when she cries
Emotions are so wide and deep
Emotions strong and true
For logic is but lost on her
React, not respond to you
She loves me sure, but it's so often
That she hates the things I do

I get angry
I feel angry
She runs away
Life turns to small talk
Our run, now a walk
Temper, temper I tell myself
Or I'll smack her across the room
Patience, patience I yell inside
I hold it until I'm blue

She loves me sure, but it's so often
That she hates the things I do

Go for it

When life seems to drag you down

And life's problems make you drown

Then you should always look around

And go for it

In its simple simple way

Questions never do obey

So you look around and say

"I'll go for it."

When life's' decisions pass you by

And all time does is fly

Don't you fret and don't you cry

Just go for it

And when seeing is not believing

You go for it

He loved by conviction.

He who lives by preference
is weaker than He who lives by conviction.

The killer that hides during the day
is often revealed by the moons hidden night.

They that give themselves over to emotion
are often times swept past all logic and cascade away.

The torments of temptation
are nothing compared to the consequence of sin.

What you do in the secret
will be revealed at the judgment seat of God.

Living in the fullness of the law
does not mean that you are just, only law-abiding.

Doing things the good way fails
Since anything that is not of faith is sin.

And he who loves by preference
is weaker than He who loves by conviction.

We want you!

Come and join the revelation
of the ultimate suffering of the Lord.
Come and see the revelation
of the wondrous glory of His word.

Feel the power pulsing onward.
Feel the steel grasp of the pull.
Come and find your body wandering.
come and die once and for all.
Join the death of your desire.
Taste of loves sweet endless fire.
Fellowship and matchless splendor.
Die to self, lose all control.

Come and join the revelation
of the ultimate suffering of the sword.
Come and see the revelation
of the awesome splendor of the Lord.

Footprints on the Hart
(The other footprints poem)

Tiny footprints
Large footprints on my heart
Footprints by lovers
Footprints by my friends
Footprints I needed
And those I did not
I have been stepped on
Kicked
Massaged by Birkenstocks
And punctured by cleats
Footprints of love
Joy, pain and laughter
I see my life
By the marks they have made
My ups and my downs
My goods and my bads
Footprints of Jesus
All over my head
Footprints of her
Alone in my bed
I know his feet
Were shod inside peace
I know those toes
Were trusted indeed
For I am not stepped on
A doormat, am not
But my heart is open
For love and for hate
Footprints you say
How common is that
A footprint is dusty
And dust gets in cracks
So every inside part

Of my life
Has been muddied
And dustied and crudied
By mud
For tears, sweat and blood
Have made the dust wet
And footprints are left
All alone in the muck
And footprints are all
That matters to me
Footprints of you
Footprints of me

Good ole' Sarah *

The star in the sky
  That thought of her first
    To the wave in the sea
      That crashed into me

From the first to the last
  Upon mountain cliffs told
    That Earth gained a fortune
      When it gained her soul

And now oceans crash
  And meteors fall
    And Heaven doth gasp
      'Cause she's moving away

"Eek!" said God
  "Quick go get the angels
    I've got five against odds
      She ends up in Las Vegas."

Essays

That One Time I Quit Protesting

Today, as I write this, I look back along the timeline of my own personal theological reformation and am amazed. I still cry at the book: The Cross and the Switchblade and I still cry at sappy movies. But most importantly, I still love Jesus with all of my being. No amount of God or any amount of the lack of God could shake me from my foundation in Him.

There is no theology than can dissuade me from standing up and seeing my mother at eye level after being prayed over in "The Name of Jesus of Nazareth." Punching people in the back... What kind of ministry was that?

I started as a Nazarene, went to a Lutheran then Mennonite School. During my school years I moved from the Charismatic, breached Pentecostalism... All before the age of 10. In High-School, I joined a Baptist church, then a Disciples of Christ church, then a Methodist church, and finally a Word of Faith church. I went to a Charismatic seminary, was almost baptized in a Russian Orthodox church, snatched a few bars from Roman Catholicism, and became Non-Denominational. As an adult, I ministered at a Vineyard, a Non-Denominational, A Christian Church Denomination church, An Assemblies of God, and another Non-Denominational.

After my first and second divorces, I began to change. I became a Deist, then Wesleyanism I became a Partial- Preternist, and finally decided to dump the Protestant movement all together. I advanced closer and closer to Greek Orthodoxy for a while but backed away and just floated along for a while, doing nothing in any church or saying that I belonged to any religion at all. My root was in the root of David, the chute of that root, Christ alone. The God of Abraham. The one Abraham called: "God Most High."

And I think that's where I am today. Religion! BAH! Suckers follow creeds. Lovers follow Christ.

You know, the only time "Religion" is mentioned in the New Testament is in the book of James?

Pure religion and undefiled before God and the Father is this:

A)   To visit the orphan and widows in their affliction
B)   To keep himself unspotted from the world

That's religion. To love people and to remain pure. And so if I do follow a "Religion" then I follow this one... The one James talks about. I'm going to call it: "The Jesus Religion" for the sake of argument. You can call it "The YHVH Religion" or "The Yahshua Religion" if you want to... That's fine. But we're all talking about the same guy. "The Intelligent Designer." The one who doesn't want us ignoring the poor and who cares about reaching all of us more than we are concerned with reaching all of the world.

That's my religion today. I love the Bible. The Tanakh is my best friend. Jesus actually became the Word and so now it's more alive than ever before. Let the minds be blown!

To be honest, if Doris Howard were to rise from the dead and come over to my house and ask me: "So... How are you with Health and Wealth?"

I just might tell her: "Jesus healed us by His stripes. He owns the cattle on a thousand hills. I suppose if He loves me, he'll give me my daily bread."

Because it's still the best answer.

Jesus is always the best answer.

Odd Heroes

And then one day in 1988 I met Doris Howard. She was the youth group leader at Central Christian Church in Wichita, Kansas. Along with Keith Malcom, Larry Albrecht and others, this became my first ecclesia... A home among believers. My parents were attending Central Community Church across town, and at the time there was not really an active youth ministry going on there. It existed, but not to the measure that Central Christian had. We used to joke about going to CCC, but not CCC. I think, in actuality the youth leader at Central Community suggested that we try out Central Christian. That was the first and best thing he ever did for me. Good guy. Thanks for sending me to Central Christian, because that's where I met Rich Mullins.

You know the guy, or at least you've heard his songs. "Awesome God" probably is the one you might know. Anyway, pretty famous singer/songwriter back in the 80's. He died tragically in 1997 but his legacy still lives on thru the children he ministered to and the music he wrote. He and his buddy Beaker would help Doris teach and sing and lead us youth into righteousness and goodness and try to find a Ragamuffin God in the Empirical World of Man… Good quest, but not the one I was on. Still, I can't help recognize his love for the Creator and the message that he brought when he sang to me and my friends. At the time musically, I was more into Minor Threat and Fugazi, but still I respected any adult that would walk around barefoot with tattered jeans and hippy hair talking about St. Francis of Assisi. I had met someone that stood outside the church and called to it, begging it to worship God with a pure heart.

What really moved my heart at Central Christian was meeting a crazy guy by the name of Frank Peretti. In 1986 he wrote a book called: "This Present Darkness" and my whole universe was thrown upside down, put into a blender and smashed into pound cake. Suddenly, this was what I had been looking for. A world where the veil between our physical reality and the spirit realm had been etched away and you could peer into the night with God's own night vision. He came and talked to our youth group, the college age, then had an autograph signing and then preached the two services on Sunday morning. I don't know how, but I managed to attend all of those sessions. If I were to model myself after anyone, this would be the guy.

And so it was, I bought This Present Darkness and then the next year bought the follow up book: Piercing the Darkness. I must have read each one three times. It's odd for me to read or watch, but these were special occasions. If there was any lesson to be had in finding a real God in the midst of Hollywood lies, this would be it. Besides, when you really get into the Bible, Hollywood ain't got nothing on it anyway. The weakest truths are always more powerful than the deepest lies. Real eyes realize real lies. So with Peretti's book in one hand and the Bible in another, I dug into both with a new fervor and zeal.

As a teenager I didn't know of anyone who had dug into angelology more than I had at that time, as the leader of the Bible Study at my school, I maybe took two or three weeks to go over the information that I had learned as I presented it to the rest of the students. I just realized how horrible that sentence was. But really, I was getting deeper and deeper into the reality of who God was and what He had actually created on this earth and just how far the rabbit hole really went. But this book isn't about angels. It's about the creation of angels, the animals, the stars and the very world itself.